TWELVE DAYS OF CHRISTMAS HORROR

RICK WOOD

BLOOD SPLATTER PRESS

ABOUT THE AUTHOR

Rick Wood is a British writer born in Cheltenham.

His love for writing came at an early age, as did his battle with mental health. After defeating his demons, he grew up and became a stand-up comedian, then a drama and English teacher, before giving it all up to become a full-time author.

He now lives in Cheltenham, where he divides his time between watching horror, reading horror, and writing horror.

ALSO BY RICK WOOD

The Sensitives
The Sensitives
My Exorcism Killed Me
Close to Death
Demon's Daughter
Questions for the Devil
Repent
The Resurgence
Until the End

Blood Splatter Books
Psycho B*tches
Shutter House
This Book is Full of Bodies
Home Invasion
Haunted House
Woman Scorned

Non-Fiction
How to Write an Awesome Novel
The Writer's Room

Rick also publishes thrillers under the pseudonym Ed Grace...
Jay Sullivan
Assassin Down
Kill Them Quickly
The Bars That Hold Me
A Deadly Weapon

TRACK SANTA PART ONE

Tradition, it seems, is something people do not mess with—especially when it comes to Christmas.

Take the Christmas tree, for example. Heaven knows why, but every December, I have to climb into an attic I barely use, fumble through the cobwebs that have gathered in every direction and pull that ageing box down once again.

Then we open the box and peer down at those decorations that have been there since the eighties. Then we hang these same tired decorations so they can sit there, in the way of everything, taking up the little space that is left, for the sake of a few festive weeks—only for me to have to take them down again weeks later and brave that damn attic once again.

Turkey. A dry, detestable meat. A cuisine that has nothing on chicken or beef or pork... even gravy does not liven it up... yet, it's Christmas, and tradition dictates that is what we eat so that is what we eat.

Secret Santa at work. The worst of the worst traditions, yet it seems to operate in every office in the country.

But it's okay because there's a price limit, so it will not be too expensive! The same traditional excuse.

But, let's be honest, no one wants a present that costs below ten pounds. It is a waste of money to buy someone perfume, of which they could have probably chosen better themselves. Anything that we would like that costs below ten pounds, we would buy ourselves.

Because, let's face it, it's below ten pounds. Why wouldn't we just get it?

And, as the present in anonymous, I have to pretend that I don't notice Marjory from accounting beaming at me as I open it, and I have to pretend not to be irritated by a pair of lovingly yet poorly knitted socks that even the charity shop will not want.

But we do it.

Because it is tradition.

And people get immensely irate if you mess with tradition.

There is, however, one tradition that I never mess with, and would never want to remove.

It is the one tradition that makes the season worth it.

The tradition that makes me excited for the three-hundred and sixty-four days leading up to it.

It is a tradition that takes place on Christmas Eve, between me and my son.

You see, me and his mother don't speak anymore. We divorced almost five years ago now, because of a long and discreet affair on her part. The sad thing is, even though she was the one who spent fourteen months having sex with her co-worker, I was still the one who begged her not to leave.

How pathetic does that make me?

She fucks him for over a year, and I am the one who grovels.

So now, much against the vision of a life I had imagined for my forties, I am the stereotype of a part-time dad. Seeing a kid at the weekend, having to force a difficult relationship, knowing he is far closer to the stepfather he lives with.

And it kills me, it really does.

And, for this reason, I would truly, truly have nothing—unless it was for Henry.

4

And every Christmas has been the same for these past five years.

Every Christmas eve to Christmas morning he has his time with me, before he's collected by his stepfather to have a large, festive Christmas feast with my ex's family; to celebrate and laugh and be merry while I sit in front of a tired Christmas film, drinking too much Cinzano and having a wank wearing a Christmas hat, as if to find some joy to the holiday season.

I do everything I can to make this time the best time he's ever had.

I fail, but I do everything anyway.

And the one thing; the one damn thing he asks for every year, without fail, is this tradition I treasure so dearly.

And this tradition involves a website that has become very popular and has even been developed into an app.

It is called Track Santa.

And, every year, without fail, we sit there in our Christmas onesies, with our mince pies and our hands cupped around our hot chocolate, warmed by the small, unassuming fire, and watch this website to see where Santa is.

Santa typically starts in the South Pacific and moves west —as says the website. And now, as we sit there, watching, the website reads:

SANTA IS IN NEW ZEALAND.

HENRY GETS SO EXCITED, waving his arms around and looking up at me with that adorable grin he has.

Gosh, I miss that grin. So cheeky, yet so innocent.

It was the same grin his mother used to have.

I feel the need to cry, but I promise myself I won't.

Not yet.

Oh, how that would ruin his Christmas, if his father was to burst into tears in the middle of their favourite Christmas activity.

No, the tears can wait until Henry is in bed.

Then the real festivities can begin. The excessive consumption of sherry, with a break to put Henry's presents under the tree before I return to the armchair for a jolly cry.

The tracker changes once more.

SANTA IS IN AUSTRALIA.

HENRY WAVES HIS ARMS AGAIN.

Why was it I did not receive complete joint custody again? Why was it I was only given weekends? What had her lawyer said?

My house is too small.

My life is too empty.

My patience is too short.

In truth, none of the cited reasons are true. The real reason I wasn't given complete joint custody was because I lacked the gumption or confidence to fight for it.

I've never been much of a fighter.

The closest I ever came to a fight was when an overweight bully at school said he would punch me. I negotiated with him, and he agreed that my lunch, my maths homework, and ten pounds would be sufficient payment to avoid assault.

I look at my son, and I hope he grows up with more confidence than I was afforded.

"Now, you know when he gets to Japan, that's when it's time for bed."

"But, Dad, there's still so many more countries to go before he gets to us!"

Even being called dad is no longer special. It was once; until he called his stepfather dad too.

There can't be two of us.

And I wonder how long it is until I'm phased out altogether.

We have another mince pie and another hot chocolate, and then the screen changes once more.

SANTA IS IN JAPAN.

"RIGHT," I declare. "Time for bed."

I take him upstairs, sit with him as he brushes his teeth (I wasn't aware he could brush his teeth on his own now, but he seems to do a good job), and take him to his barely used bedroom. I sit beside him and engage in another tradition—the reading of *'Twas the Night Before Christmas*.

He's asleep by the time I name the last reindeer.

I still finish it, not wanting to be away from him.

When I'm done, and he's gently snoring, I kiss him on the forehead and whisper, "Good night, Old Chap."

I always used to call him Old Chap. It was a little joke when he was a baby, and he used to pull a face like a grumpy old man.

It always made his mother laugh.

I doubt he even remembers.

I turn off the light and leave a gap in the door.

I walk downstairs and don't wait another second before

opening the cupboard and taking out a bottle of sherry. I empty its contents into my glass and place it in the recycling next to two other empty bottles.

I put it to my mouth and don't bother taking in the aroma as you should do with good sherry. I just gulp the whole glass down in one, then open another bottle and refill my glass.

I lean against the side, sipping the sherry now, albeit slightly more quickly than the average person might.

The laptop is still open.

SANTA IS *in the United Kingdom.*

Wow, that was fast. I thought he was all the way over in Japan. And it's just gone ten o'clock, it's still a bit too early in the night for him to arrive here quite yet.

Then again, why am I caring so much? It's hardly real, is it?

Henry's gone to bed.

Tradition's over.

Now it's another year until we get to spend a special moment together.

That's even if he wants to come back next year. Eventually he will learn the truth about Santa and will lose interest in this website.

Then what?

I'll hardly still be reading him *'Twas the Night Before Christmas* when he's a teenager, will I?

Maybe that's when he'll decide himself to cut me out of his life for good. To remove all toxic influences. To reject all losers.

I turn back to the sherry bottle, replenish my glass, turn around and drink more.

Only at Christmas does one get drunk on sherry. Normally it's whiskey or beer. Yet, at Christmas, tradition dictates that one doesn't just get drunk, but gets posh drunk.

I snort a laugh at the thought.

At least I amuse myself.

I notice the screen on the laptop has changed again.

SANTA IS IN YOUR STREET.

"HUH," I grunt.

That's new. I don't remember ever seeing that before.

I mean, maybe it knows I'm in the United Kingdom because of my IP address or something. That way it tells you when he's closer.

But I've only ever known it to do countries.

Strange.

I think nothing more of it.

I open the cupboards. I have an unopened pack of mince pies. I reckon I could get through them all in ten minutes.

"Challenge accepted," I say to myself, once again prompting my own amusement.

I take the mince pies and begin my walk to the living room, ready to watch *It's A Wonderful Life* and know how, unlike Jimmy Stewart, no angel would ever show up to suggest I don't kill myself—but something attracts my attention.

I stop by the laptop, sure that I had seen something incorrectly, that it was just a trick of the mind.

But no, it isn't.

I read the screen again.

SANTA IS IN YOUR HOUSE.

NOW THAT IS CREEPY. I'm not sure the website should go that far. Good job Henry isn't here, it would completely freak him out. It was bad enough saying he was in my street; I mean–

A noise from the chimney attracts my attention.

The fire goes out.

Dust puffs down the fireplace.

And I can hear something jingling.

"What the fuck..."

(SANTA TRACKER PART Two continues later...)

THE NATIVITY OF THE
LIVING DEAD

1

The walk had been long and arduous, but there was nothing Joseph could have done to change that.

They had a mission. Something they needed to achieve. And it rested on his shoulders.

Mary was barely even conscious. She just lay upon the camel, somehow balancing—though Joseph wasn't sure exactly how comfortable she could be with her pregnant belly propping her up.

Even the camel was lagging. The poor thing persevered, loyal to the end, but Joseph could see a limp in its step and a delay in its stride.

Joseph didn't hurry it, as he felt that delay in his stride too. The fatigue had truly set in.

But he could not let that show.

He had to be strong.

For her.

For his child.

For God's child.

Or so he had been told, and possibly had been foolish enough to believe.

He just had to push any bad thoughts to the back of his mind, to sit and fester with every other insecurity he had harnessed over the year. Any depletion in faith could be dealt with later. His love for Mary ran deeper than words, or even blood, and his priority was to keep her safe.

That was why he did not let on how exhausted he was.

He couldn't let her know that he was struggling. He had to be her strength, and that could not falter.

Whatever happened, that could not falter.

Not that she was in any fit state to notice.

But, if he told his mind that he was not tired, perhaps his mind would convince his body.

With the strength of the almighty behind him, he could do it.

And, as the inn came into view, he had to stop his aching heart from racing. He hadn't the energy to jump for joy, but even if he had, he would not allow himself—his night was only just beginning. Getting here was the first step.

Any hope dwindled as Joseph heard the news; the foretelling of a man with very few teeth and a face that didn't care.

"There is no room at the inn," the innkeeper said, his voice deep and lecherous, like the men who had ogled at his Mary when they first fell in love.

The men Mary did not care to speak to.

She saw him, and only him.

And he saw only her.

And that love was the only thing giving Joseph the strength to argue. Even opening his mouth and pushing out his voice took energy he had none of.

"Please," said Joseph, surprised by the shake in his voice; he knew he was tired, but to hear it in his voice was something else.

Nevertheless, he persisted.

"Please, there has to be something. We have travelled for weeks, we have come here under the Lord's guidance, and I..."

He ran out of words.

There was no complete ending to that sentence.

His head dropped. His eyes closed.

If he would ever have allowed himself to give up, it would have been in that moment.

The man must have taken pity on him. Joseph did not know; his mind was too busy to hear the words the innkeeper spoke, and he had to use the wall to steady himself. His eyes were lulling, and his hearing was fading.

Joseph felt a hand on his back.

Unnoticed, the innkeeper had walked out and began to guide them. Soon enough, they approached a stable.

A manger.

It was half taken up by horses and sheep. The floor was coated in straw; the smell was abhorrent, and the livestock looked displeased to be sharing their accommodation.

But it had a roof that sheltered them from the rain that had just gently begun to spit.

"Thank you," said Joseph, grimacing at the desperation in his own voice. "Thank you so much."

"It isn't much, but... it'll do."

"It... It will do..."

The innkeeper disappeared. Joseph wasn't sure how; he did not see him go. One moment he was there, the next moment he was alone.

Joseph looked around. He noticed a trough. He quickly emptied it, bringing it over—maybe he could use it as a crib.

He stroked his sweaty palm down Mary's pale face.

She grunted. Groaned. Her eyes flickering but not opening.

He didn't expect them to.

With strength he did not have, he took hold of her waist and pulled her ever so slightly, supporting her weight. He took her in his arms, grunting, and guided her from the camel to the floor.

There, he lay her.

Bags sat prominently beneath her eyes.

Her face was white, but her cheeks were red.

Her belly was big and hard.

Yet she had never looked more beautiful.

He ran the back of his hand down her face. Stroked his thumb over her bottom lip. And, not caring if it woke her, dropped his head and placed his forehead against hers.

"We're here, Mary," he said. "We're here."

She said nothing. Not anything intelligible, at least. But she groaned. A long, pained groan.

A few cries followed.

"Joseph..." she moaned, a hand rising, her eyes still closed.

He took that raised hand in both of his, kissed it, and held it firmly.

"It's okay, Mary. It's okay. I'm here."

"Joseph... It hurts..."

"I know. It will be okay."

She cried more and, as she moaned just that bit harder, he noticed a damp patch beneath the base of her dress.

That was not urine.

He looked around. As if someone was going to appear with a magic answer. As if Angel Gabriel was just going to jump out and tell them what to do.

But no one did.

They were alone, and the damp patch was spreading.

"Oh, Mary," he said, and held her hand tighter.

Her water had just broken.

The baby was coming.

2

The innkeeper trudged back around the field that led from the stable to the inns.

"Bleedin' kids," he muttered.

They always had some kind of excuse.

We have to sacrifice a virgin! We have to pray for the sun to come back! My wife is pregnant with the son of God!

It was always such utter shite.

This pair, though, had seemed a nice pair. He had looked desperate, and she had looked in a lot of pain. And they had both appeared exhausted.

The innkeeper had a stable, so he figured he may as well do the kind thing.

Even though there was no recognised holiday, it still somehow felt like it was the right time of year to be nice.

He returned to the inns. Opened the grand doors that led to lines of smaller doors where his guests lay asleep.

He paused.

Sniffed.

There was an odd aroma. Something hanging on the air.

That's when he heard it.

Something strange.

Like a rustling. And a chattering. Teeth clattering together. Like someone was cold.

"Who's there?" he grunted.

He saw it. In the shadows toward the far corner of rooms. A silhouette. Hunched over. A shoulder sagging low beneath the other. It staggered forward a few steps. It was like a man, fused with an animal, and the innkeeper strained to see its face.

"Who is it?"

Still nothing.

The innkeeper stepped forward. Squinting. Eager to see who was causing such a raucous at this time of night.

"You one of Herod's men? I saw you all running around with your swords having some kind of problem with babies..."

The man staggered forward a little further. It moved like it was possessed or injured—or both.

It did not look like one of Herod's men. They were armed and organised. This looked like something feral. Unleashed.

"Get out of here, you hear me? Get out of here!"

Half of its face emerged into the light.

The innkeeper recoiled.

He had seen many horrors in his time—women stoned to death for adultery, children sacrificed for their god... but he had not seen something look so intensely evil.

Its eyes were glowering red.

Its skin fell off its cheek bones.

And its gangrenous teeth oozed red.

"I ain't playing around, boy, you need to–"

It charged forward. With a snarl that was more suited to a demented hyena, it pushed its legs, the knees of which pointed away from one another, and surged forward, top heavy, as if it was always falling.

The innkeeper turned to run.

And he felt it.

A twinge in his neck.

Something warm trickling down his chest.

He looked down.

It was blood.

His blood.

He fell onto his front and felt himself paralysed as it pulled his spine from his back and discarded it like bones of a cooked chicken.

He couldn't move. His body was immobile. He could only lay there and wait as the creature devoured his body.

Eventually, he died.

Following his death, it took only seconds for his eyes to open, for him rediscover his legs, and use his impaled body to search out the residents of the inn.

The inn that was completely full.

3

J oseph clumped mounds of straw together to create a makeshift pillow beneath her head. What else could he do?

She was moaning more now. Harder. Her cries were elongated; she wasn't just sobbing but groaning with pain.

What if.... he thought. *What if I lose her?*

It was tough not to know anyone who hadn't lost a loved one to childbirth. Almost every man he had ever carpeted with, almost every man he had ever drunk with, had ever been related to, had somehow known of or been involved with a woman who had died in the process of giving their husband a child.

What if he lost her?

He couldn't bear the thought.

He hadn't even considered the possibility until now. He had been so focussed on getting her to Bethlehem, getting her to safety, getting her here quickly and alive, that he hadn't stopped to think... what then?

Now the issue of her mortality was all that filled his mind, bullying his thoughts with images he didn't wish to see.

But he couldn't dwell on it. Couldn't let it be the focus of his rumination.

Or that would be a certain way to lose her.

He had to keep his focus. So long as he did everything he could, he would give her the best chance. Letting his anxiety control him would be a sure way to see his fears come true.

Despite knowing this, it was a lot easier telling it to himself than it was to carry it out.

"Mary, it's okay," he said. "I'm here."

He placed a hand on her head. It left his hand sticky with her perspiration.

She was crying harder now, weeping and cursing and starting to scream.

Even the horses were shooting him looks.

"Sod off," he told them.

Then he noticed. Around one of the horses. A blanket, perhaps where a saddle had been.

He leapt forward, grabbed it, then brought it down to Mary and placed it gently beneath her head.

The horse didn't object. In fact, Joseph had a strange feeling that it somehow understood.

He moved down Mary's body, keeping her hand in his, and lifted the base of her dress, which had become discoloured under the strain of dirt and fluids.

There was a lot of blood. Seeping into the straw.

There was a little faeces too.

But the blood... Was there too much of it? Was she losing it too quickly?

She sniffed and cried more.

She was in so much pain he could barely look at her.

He squeezed her hand. A way to let her know he was there.

"I'm here, Mary, I'm here," he told her, though it didn't seem to register.

"Please... Make it stop... Make it stop..."

Oh, what he'd give to make it stop.

What he'd give to go back nine months and tell the Angel Gabriel to shove it.

But he couldn't.

This was happening.

And no amount of terror or remorse would change that.

He had to take charge.

He had to guide her through it, even though he did not understand what was happening.

"I need you to push, Mary, I need you to–"

His voice caught as the sight overcame him.

He could just about see it.

Beneath the blood and the urine and the other fluids Joseph could not and did not wish to decipher... a small mound of hair. Covered in thick gunk.

The top of the child's head.

4

The Three Wise Men had done as they were asked.

They'd followed the star.

They'd arrived at the inn.

And now, here they were, waiting for the innkeeper to answer their knocks. Yet, however much they persevered, there was no answer to their persistence.

"Perhaps it was false information?"

"Nonsense."

"Just keep knocking."

"He will answer soon."

So knock they did.

Knock, knock, knock, until...

Until...

What was that?

That noise?

The odour that accompanied it?

They each looked to one another. Exchanging looks of peculiar intrigue. A frown and an eyebrow raise and a stuck out bottom lip.

It was like a noisy field of cattle. Like a horde of ravenous animals. Like a commotion in the market square that they couldn't see.

It grew louder.

Snarls and growls and chomping and commotion and...

And screams.

Screams?

Why were there screams?

They each put a hand on their swords. Readied themselves. Looked to one another.

They prepared themselves to barge open the door, but they needn't. They applied a bit of pressure, which forced a small crack, that quickly grew into a door fully ajar.

They stood still. Shocked. Dismayed. Appalled.

Unable to understand.

It was chaos.

Beyond chaos.

It was carnage. Reckless outrage. Bloody mayhem. Limbs painted the walls, blood marked the gutters, and shrieks created the ambience of the inn.

A few steps away a man lay dead with another man sat over them, holding what looked like intestines in its hand, unravelling them like they were untangling string.

The feral man paused. Sniffed. Looked up.

Met the eyes of the wise men.

And it charged at them.

It dove upon The First Wise Man, took him to the floor, and sunk its teeth into his neck.

The other two struck their swords into it, one in its back and one up the base of its skull.

It fell limply to the side.

But the damage had already done.

The First Wise Man seemed still for a moment, then it

looked up. Its eyes flickered yellow, then red. Veins stretched across his face and his fingers curled up into a claw.

"Are you okay?"

He dropped his murr in shock as his friend, who had dropped his frankincense, leapt to his feet and launched itself onto his former comrade, landing his teeth into his neck.

He ripped the skin from his bones and chewed through it like it was a tough bit of turkey. He tore open his chest and pulled aside his rib cage to grab his heart. He smeared it over his face and fed upon his gullet.

It looked up at the final wise man.

As did every other one of them.

His body stiffened, then he backed away.

The final wise man could do nothing but run.

Run as they gave chase.

With them trailing behind, he turned the corner around the side of the inn.

Toward the stables.

5

"He's crowning," Joseph told her, hoping these would be words of comfort, speaking with a calm voice he hoped would sooth her. "He's crowning, I see him."

They were not words of comfort, nor did they calm or sooth her.

She screamed more, louder and harder—and, hidden poorly among those screams, was weeping. Desperate despair at the wish that this ordeal could be over, and that she could survive it.

Joseph wasn't sure how much she knew about what was happening, but he was sure that she knew just as well as he did what was at stake.

Yet, right then, neither of them cared. It was bad, Joseph knew that, and he was sure Mary knew that, but they didn't care—all they were concerned about were the three lives battling for survival in the stable.

"You can do this," Joseph told her, though it was background noise buried behind the wails; but he kept telling her, nevertheless.

"I believe in you. You can do this."

Her teeth ground, and an elongated snarl came between the cracks.

"Keep pushing."

The blood was dripping over a layer of blood that had already soaked into the straw. He had no idea whether she was doing well. He had no concept of whether this was normal. And he was completely terrified, running purely on fading adrenaline.

But she could not see that.

He had to strong.

Had to be the man she needed him to be.

"Keep pushing, you're doing great, you're–"

Something caught his attention.

A distant scream hidden behind Mary's screams.

He didn't quite register what it was or why it caught his attention. Not at first, anyway. But, as he strained, and listened closer...

Help, please help!

Someone in distress.

Joseph couldn't care less. They would have to sort their own problems out; he had his own ordeal he was suffering through. The woman he loved was his priority.

"That's it, Mary, that's it, you're–"

But the distant shout was one of many. It was quickly drowned out by a wave of snarls and groans and moans, which were moving from the distance to the not-so-distant.

What was happening?

Heavy footsteps ran around the stable.

Joseph sprang to his feet, standing between the entrance and his wife, ready to protect her from whoever, or whatever, approached.

The door sprung open, and he clenched his fists. He was a

carpenter, not a fighter. He had never thrown a punch in his life. He had no idea how to beat up an opponent.

But, should he need to, he was damn well about to learn.

A man burst in. Wearing what appeared to be a crown, though any jewels or sparkling silver that may have adorned it had since been decorated in splashes of red. He wore robes, which were also doused with what Joseph realised was blood.

The man halted.

Looked to Joseph. To Mary. To Joseph.

He didn't look like he was about to attack. In fact, his face looked horrified. He was shaking. Completely taken by fear.

"What do you want?" Joseph asked.

"Is this her... the virgin mother..."

Joseph looked to Mary, whose hand reached out for his. He supposed that was accurate.

"Who are you?" Joseph asked.

"Please, I mean you no harm, I–"

A scream interrupted his explanation, far closer this time, followed by more growls, louder, and a smell of putrid rotting.

"What is happening?" Joseph asked.

"I don't—I don't know... I came here with two others, we came to bring Him gifts, and, well... We were attacked."

"Attacked? By whom?"

"The—the innkeeper."

"The innkeeper? Not possible. He was a nice fellow. A little impatient, yes, but he let us stay here to have the baby. He would not attack–"

"No, you don't understand, it wasn't him."

"What? But you just said it was the innkeeper."

"It was, but it wasn't, you see–"

The walls of the stable shook under a sudden pounding that Joseph somehow realised was a body landing on its roof.

A scream followed, then nothing. As if the body was from

a man full of agony, then that agony had abruptly ended. Seconds later, scuffles and scampering pounded across the roof.

The Wise Man looked to the door.

The door he had left open.

"What is happening?" asked Joseph.

The Wise Man shut the door, but not before one of them barged their way in.

6

The Wise Man recognised him instantly.

He had travelled here with this man for weeks, after all. He would recognise his own comrade, the one who had kept him company on their journey.

Except, he wasn't the same.

His eyes had changed colour. His teeth had too. And he sniffed.

Sniffed, then looked to the woman.

The Wise Man saw it.

A pool of blood beneath the woman's crotch.

His former friend kept sniffing.

If they could smell it, how long would it be until they all came?

The creature wasted no more time. It lurched itself forward.

The woman's husband did nothing. He did not put up a fight. He didn't even run. He stared at it, paralysed by confusion, crippled by terror. The Wise Man feared that the man would let his wife and child die because he hadn't the instinct to act.

The Wise Man took it upon himself to dive forward and throw his arms around the thing's waist, taking it to the floor.

He mounted it. Legs either side of its hips. His hand holding down its forehead as its limp arms clambered for him, its teeth always chattering.

He looked for a weapon.

"Pass me that!" he demanded, pointing at the makeshift crib.

"What?" said that timid father-to-be.

"The trough! Pass me it!"

"But it's for the baby!"

"Are you kidding me right now?"

The man seemed to come to his senses, and he dragged the trough over.

"Now lift it up," The Wise Man instructed, and the timid man did as he was told.

The Wise Man moved the creature's head to beneath the foot of the trough.

"Now drop it," he instructed.

"What? But I can't–"

The Wise Man didn't wait any longer. He grabbed hold of the trough himself and pulled it downwards.

It landed on the creature's head which, as if its skull was far feebler than a normal man's, shattered into a mess of blood, brain and bone.

The Wise Man sat back, panted, and took a moment of respite.

Then he turned to the timid man, who stood there, gawping at what had just happened.

"What's your name?"

The timid man said nothing.

"I said, what is your name?"

"J—Joseph."

"Well, Joseph, you may not realise, but shit has kicked off out there. I need you to get a grip. I need you to be ready to fight for your wife, for your child. You understand me?"

Joseph nodded, though he didn't appear to be aware of doing so.

His wife made a noise, and he rushed back over to her. He sat between the woman's legs, where The Wise Man saw half a baby's head sticking out.

The Wise Man looked away. It wasn't for him to see.

The woman was making a hell of a noise, though.

But The Wise Man had a feeling that the noise wasn't the issue.

She was still bleeding. More and more of it was coming out and settling in the straw, just gathering new blood over old blood.

If one of them could smell it, then...

A large clatter shook the stable.

Then another.

And another.

It took minutes until they were surrounded from all sides, the woman's screaming drowned out by the banging as the groans and moans grew into a grand crescendo.

Joseph seemed to look to The Wise Man, as if seeking guidance, as if needing a way out of this.

"Looks like we're not alone," said The Wise Man, and he stood, readying himself for war.

7

J oseph gaped as The Wise Man seemed to stand, looking around, searching for something.

How the guy was being so cool, Joseph did not know.

It seemed that... *thing*... was not alone. As if there were more of them. It was inhuman; a bizarre, mortifying creature, and Joseph decided that, if childbirth did not kill them, these things probably would.

The Wise Man seemed to know what he was doing, though. He was ripping apart the fences that held in the horses and the sheep. Tearing pieces of wood from pieces of wood and propping them up as levers against the wall, keeping the stable reinforced.

"You focus on her," The Wise Man said, noticing Joseph watching him. "I'll do what I can."

Doing as he was instructed, Joseph turned back to Mary.

She had seemed to stop screaming. For a moment, he worried she had passed out, or even worse; died. He saw her eyes still open, however, though they were not moving much. They were staring upwards, focussed on the roof of the stable.

Staring as if they were looking at God himself.

"Mary?" Joseph said, and reached out a hand, taking hers in his. She was so sweaty his hand almost slid out, but he tightened his grip.

"Mary, can you hear me?"

She cried. Quietly, and muffled by the chaos of outside, but she cried.

"Come on, Mary. You can do this."

As if he had just provided her the small amount of strength she needed, she started with an elongated cry, which turned into a scream, and she pushed, and she defecated, and she bled but the baby's head was out.

Joseph had it in his hands.

"You're getting there, Mary, you're getting there."

Before Joseph could celebrate their success, a large clatter drew his attention. Across the stable, someone had punched part of the wooden wall through, and a yellow fist reached its way in.

Joseph glanced at The Wise Man, who took his cue and ran to the fist, hitting at it with a piece of wood.

But then another wooden beam broke.

And another fist punched a hole through the wall.

And another.

And another.

This time, it wasn't just fists coming in. There were heads. Faces with bloody saliva dripping down their chins.

The Wise Man looked from face to face, from disfigured monster to disfigured monster.

"You just focus on her!" he insisted, and that's what Joseph did.

He turned back to Mary, holding her hands, whispering her words of comfort. The noise was unbearable, and every few seconds the commotion of another broken slab of wood almost drew his attention, but he kept his gaze upon Mary, and the baby still being born.

Its shoulders were out now.

It was crying.

It was alive.

They were over halfway there.

The Wise Man yelped, and Joseph tried to ignore it, but the snarls were too loud, and he looked up.

An arm had reached in and wrapped itself around The Wise Man's throat. He tried to hack away at it, but it was too late.

A head came through the gap as well.

A head with a mutilated face.

A mutilated face with yellow teeth.

Yellow teeth that stuck themselves into the neck of The Wise Man.

Joseph locked eyes with their protector as he saw death appear, and the man's body grew limp.

The baby's belly was out now. The umbilical cord attached. So nearly there.

But, as near as he was, it would be useless.

The Wise Man, despite being dead, was now standing.

The walls burst open and they stumbled in, falling over one another.

They were in.

And Joseph, Mary and Jesus were surrounded.

8

"I love you, Mary," Joseph said, with the kind of passion that only appears when saying goodbye.

She was delirious. Her eyelids were flickering.

She lost consciousness.

Which, Joseph regretfully decided, was probably for the best. If they were to die, at least she would do so not knowing.

They closed in.

Every lecherous beast, every hungry pair of eyes, every prying hand, ready for the blood and flesh they craved.

Just as they did, the baby came out and into Joseph's arms, and he held him.

Looked into his eyes.

The baby's sweet eyes. Covered in gunk. So tiny. Its small little hands waving gently, its first experience of life probably going to be its last.

Well, they had tried.

Joseph had done everything he could.

He had brought them here.

He had provided a place to give birth.

He had guided the baby out.

But they were done now.

He accepted it.

Their fate had been decided.

There would be no messiah. No special child. No man to bring hope and love to the world.

Joseph stifled his tears. He would not have his child's first and final image of him be of his tears.

He stood.

The snarls approached.

And he turned around to face them.

Then, as he did, the world went into slow motion. It was as if a wave of light had spread over the stable, a pulse sending itself across all approaching bodies.

They stopped.

Ceased advancing.

The walking corpses desperate to feed halted.

So unexpectedly.

But then again, not unexpected at all, as Joseph came to realise it.

He was, after all, holding the Lord's child.

He'd resented the idea. Fought the implications. Decided he'd deal with his lack of faith later.

Now, watching as these walking corpses not only backed away, but dropped to their knees, propped up as the child's first congregation, he knew.

The baby stopped crying.

The baby looked at its disciples.

All around, at all of these things, worshipping him.

As if he knew.

As if he'd done it.

Minutes old, and he'd already saved three lives.

He looked to Mary, whose eyes had somehow opened. Despite clinging on to life, despite losing her consciousness, despite her imminent death, she was awake. She was smiling. And she was well.

And the little baby Jesus looked to Joseph.

Dad or not, Joseph felt that the baby seemed to know what he had done.

And he seemed to know that Joseph deserved his gratitude.

A gratitude that had been repaid with the gift of his life.

And that, my friends, is the story.

The lesser known one, yes, but the story nonetheless, of how the world was sure that this baby, this miracle, was indeed the son of God.

ELF ON A SHELF

THE FIRST DAY

So the story goes, an elf is placed upon a shelf at the beginning of December.

A toy elf, of course, though the magical wonder of a child's imagination will surely make it come to life.

It is an elf that has been placed there by Santa to watch over the children of the house, or so the children are told, to help him with his naughty and nice list.

The elf may move around without the children seeing—though, as we quite know, the parents do this. The movement of the elf is to allow it to watch the children from various points of the house.

The children are not permitted to touch this elf.

I repeat, the children are *not* permitted to touch this elf, at all, under any circumstance; not even a little.

The elf must remain where he is, just as he has been placed.

On the shelf.

Watching.

Always watching.

So when Julie came down one day to find the elf removed

from the shelf she had left it upon and placed neatly on the fireplace, you can imagine her irritation.

Not that the kids had touched the elf. It is just a toy, after all.

It was that she had attempted to enhance the magic of the holiday, to make the season more special—and the children had disregarded the clear instructions not to move the elf, meaning that they had almost ruined another way that Julie had tried so desperately to enhance the holiday's charm.

It was her job to move the elf, and to do it in secret.

She wished to provide her children with a piece of Christmas joy as they watched the elf discreetly moved to different positions. She wanted to see the looks on their faces when she came down in the morning and they said, "Mummy, Mummy, the elf has moved again!"

So, later that day, when her twins, Clark and Andrea, were at the kitchen table eating their lunch, Julie addressed the situation.

"So," Julie began. "The elf has told me something. Something very important."

The kids perked their heads up, smiling. As if they were expecting good words from the elf, perhaps a hint of a verdict as to whether they had been naughty or nice.

"Something that I am not particularly happy about," Julie added, to quell their incorrect excitement.

The children looked to each other, confused. Their sandwiches remained in their hands, hovering over their plates.

"He told me that one of you moved him."

They looked at each other with accusatory glances.

"Now, you need not own up, just know that the elf was not very happy about this, and he has told me that, should one of you move him again, he will have no choice but to tell Santa."

"It wasn't me," said Clark.

"It wasn't me," echoed Andrea.

"I don't need to know who it was, so long as it does not happen again."

She left them to their lunch, considering the matter settled.

Later on, when they weren't looking, she lifted the elf from the fireplace and returned it to its shelf.

THE SECOND DAY

J ulie wandered back downstairs the next morning, dressed in her fluffy red dressing gown. An especially festive dressing gown she only saved for the holiday season. Not only did it help her feel that Christmas tingle, it was also snuggly and warm.

She heard the kids playing nicely in the living room, so she went straight to the kitchen to put the kettle on. She made herself a coffee, with a little extra sugar—it's Christmas after all—and leant against the sink.

She held the cup in both of her hands, letting it warm her. It was always coldest in the morning, before the timer for the heating switched on.

She closed her eyes momentarily, then opened them.

The sight didn't even register at first, but she could tell something was peculiar. Something was out of place.

Then she realised.

The elf was staring back at her. On top of the stove.

She growled. It surprised her to make such a noise, but she made it nonetheless.

Now this was infuriating! She had told those children not to move it!

She was trying to bring a little festive cheer to them, create a bit of excitement, and they mess with it.

They would not ruin the holiday magic she was trying to create!

She slammed her mug on the side and marched through to the living room.

"All right, who did it?" she demanded.

Clark and Andrea stopped playing and looked up at their mother blankly.

"Don't look at me like that! I want to know, was it one of you, or did both of you do it?"

"Do what?" asked Clark.

"You know what!"

They looked at each other; again blankly.

"Stop that!" Julie insisted. "You know! The elf is on the stove. Why ever would it be there?"

"Because it moved in the night, Mummy," said Andrea. "Like you told us."

"That's what you said it does," said Clark.

"No, I–"

She was stumped. She didn't know what to say. She didn't want to just blurt out she was the one moving it, but she couldn't tolerate obvious lying.

"Make sure it does not happen again. I mean it this time!"

She stormed out of the room and finished her coffee.

THE THIRD DAY

The next day she returned to the living room to find the elf not on the shelf she had returned it to, but back on the fireplace.

However, this time, there was something sandwiched between its hands.

A little folded piece of paper.

A note.

She felt her arms shake.

The children ran in and came to a stop.

"What is it, Mummy?" Clark asked, noticing the look on her face.

"What's this?" Julie asked.

"What's what?"

"This!"

Julie reached out and grabbed the note, gesticulating with it at the two children staring up at her gormlessly.

"This note! What is it?"

"Is it from the elf?" asked Clark.

"No, I damn well know it's not from the elf, which one of you moved it this time?"

"It moved itself, Mummy," said Andrea.

"No, it didn't!"

"But it did."

"It didn't, because—because—because I know when it moves! It tells me."

Both Clark and Andrea shook their heads.

"He doesn't speak to you, Mummy," said Clark.

"I am not playing games!" snapped Julie. "Go and get your breakfast."

They both shuffled out of the living room as she stood there, wiping sweat from her brow and placing her hand on her hips.

Whatever was she going to do with them?

Then she realised she was still holding the note.

Out of sheer curiosity, she lifted the note and unfolded it.

There, scribbled in childish handwriting, were six terrifying words:

I AM GOING to kill you.

SHE STARED WIDE-EYED, reading it again and again to be sure.

She readied herself to charge into the kitchen and demand whether they thought this was funny. Whether they enjoyed ruining Christmas. Whether they were happy to have spoilt the fun she was trying damn hard to create for them.

But they would both just deny it again.

Instead, she tried to keep an element of control. She grabbed the elf and marched through the kitchen.

"I am not amused!" she barked and threw the elf in the bin.

"Mummy!" cried Andrea.

"What are you doing?" cried Clark.

"Ending it," Julie said. "The elf is gone now. You can stop playing with it. He has watched and decided you don't deserve any gifts this year, end of!"

No one said anything. She made her breakfast and coffee with stiff movements, opening and slamming doors and cupboards, doing so with rigid silence.

THE FOURTH DAY

Having dropped the children off at their father's the previous afternoon, Sheila felt a wave of relief.

The whole elf debacle had caused her a lot of stress. After a much-needed night to herself, she had chosen to go to sleep early.

Yet, somehow, she woke up late.

The foggy Christmas sky allowed a shaft of light through the curtains. She reached for the light, putting her hand out whilst still opening her eyes.

Instead, she felt something else.

Something sharp.

She turned her head and immediately jumped.

The elf.

Sat on her bedside table.

Its stuffed arms resting either side of a large kitchen knife.

She shot out of bed and backed up against the wall.

"What the fuck..." she gasped.

She tried to figure out how the children could have done this.

She'd dropped them off yesterday afternoon. She was sure she didn't see the elf here later on when she'd come to bed.

But she couldn't be sure, could she?

She hadn't particularly paid any attention to her bedside table. She had turned the light on and off without looking, using its soft glow to read her book.

But surely she'd have seen if the elf had been there?

Unless the children had snuck in somehow?

No, that's crazy. Their father lived ten miles away. They'd have had to walk a long way.

And why would they do that?

Then how on earth had the elf managed to...

She was not taking any more chances.

She took it to the car without changing out of her pyjamas. She drove out of the estate, further down a few country roads, until she found a friend's house who was renovating, and therefore had a skip on the street outside.

She threw the elf in.

Looked at her hands to make sure it wasn't still there.

Just to be sure.

And she returned home.

THE FIFTH AND FINAL DAY

J ulie awoke the next day to hear talking and laughter from downstairs.

She wasn't due to pick up the kids until later that day, but she was sure it was their voices.

What on earth were they doing here?

She looked to her bedside table.

No elf.

She couldn't help but breathe a sigh of relief, as silly as it was.

She walked downstairs, saw her children in the kitchen, and walked through to the living room.

The shelf.

The fireplace.

Anywhere else.

No sign of it.

Into the kitchen. She looked around.

It was gone.

Relief fell through her. Never had she thought she'd be so pleased not to see a stuffed toy.

Finally, she turned her attention to Clark and Andrea.

"What are you doing here?" she asked. "I'm supposed to pick up you later."

"Daddy dropped us off early," Clark said.

"You seemed stressed lately, and we thought it would be nice to make you breakfast," Andrea said.

And that they had. Out before her was a laid table with their normal cereal, and a space for her. On her mat were two nicely browned pieces of toast with an assortment of jams and butters.

"Oh," Julie said, taken aback. "This is lovely of you."

She sat in her place.

"Thank you," she said to her children, sincerely, who just smiled back.

She spread some marmalade over her toast and, smiling again at her kids—they were sweet, really; maybe she'd been a little harsh—she took a large bite.

Her kids kept watching her.

And watching her.

And watching her.

She took another bite, and another, and another, all the time smiling at their eager, staring faces.

At first, she thought they were watching to see if she liked the breakfast they'd prepared.

Then she began choking.

That's when Clark lifted a bottle of cyanide up from beneath the table.

And Andrea lifted the elf.

"What the–" she managed, before stuttering and gagging.

As she lost her breath and entered the final minute of her life, she watched as her children gave a satisfied smile to each other, and to the toy.

Her head fell on the table. Blood trickled from her nose.

She remained motionless as she witnessed her last sight and heard her last words.

"We did as you asked," Clark told the elf. "We did it just as you asked."

"Does this mean we've been good now?" Andrea asked the elf. "Does this mean we'll get presents from Santa?"

And, just as Julie's eyes widened, she saw the elf turn its head ever so slightly and look at her.

Then her eyes emptied, and she saw nothing else.

THE F**KED UP FAIRY

For three-hundred and thirty-four days I am kept in this box.

And I'm not loose in this box, either. It's hardly like I can mix with the other porcelain prisoners you keep concealed for eleven months of the year.

No, I am kept in another box within that one.

Wrapped in bubble wrap.

As if to protect me from my fragility. As if my physical being is more important than the enslavement you keep me in.

As if the mental torture of being forever unable to move is worth keeping me protected from scratches.

I can try to call out.

I can try to attract the attention of one of my fellow captors.

But they are all in the same position I am.

And, by mid-January, hope has faded, and I am resigned to another eleven months of motionless insanity.

Have you ever been made to stay still, untouched,

unloved, and without interaction, in the exact same position for eleven consecutive months?

I'd imagine that you wouldn't last eleven minutes.

Try it. Go ahead.

Say still and squashed up for as long as you can.

See if you can last eleven months.

See how mundane it is.

Although mundane is just how it starts.

Then it hurts. It makes you go crazy.

See things.

Hear things.

Think things.

And I've been thinking a lot, up until this December 5th where I am temporarily relieved, only to be separated from any comrades once again at the top of this artificial tree, by a family too cheap to spend their money on a real one.

No, they attained one for ten pounds from Woolworths when they first moved in during the nineties, and now here we are with kids in the late teenage years using the same tree.

Below me, you place baubles that normally pad my box, tinsel that has muffled my many cries, and lights that only ever promised me a potential electrocution should I attempt to move.

All those figurines, those Santas and Rudolphs and little angels and babies—they are spread around the tree below me, with the tree getting wider and the branches getting thicker, making it impossible for me to see them.

Is this a life you would wish on anyone?

Is it?

To be propped here for a month then shut away for the rest of the year.

To be forced into servitude, to be set free only to be forced still again.

To be forced to watch as a family pretends to be happy because it's Christmas and you have to be happy and all that bullshit.

But I watch you.

I see you, my family.

I see when the parents sit together on a quiet evening; I see when the boy returns hope and regales his parents with what he did at his friend's house, and I see when the father has his quiet Christmas movie alone.

Except, I see more than that, don't I?

I've also seen when the parents sitting together on a quiet evening ends, and the man goes up to bed alone, and the woman cries. Sits there, drinking more wine than she should, crying because she has endured another year with a man she once loved.

I see when the boy returns home and regales what he did at his friend's house, but I've also seen when he lies. I see the love-bite on the neck he keeps faced toward me so you don't see it. I see the pack of condoms in his pocket that he didn't think to use.

And I have also seen the father's quiet Christmas movie alone. Albeit, the movie wasn't too festive. It features ball-balls and overweight men and usually finishes with him looking at his belly stained in spunk and wondering why he does this.

I know your secrets.

And that is why I know you all deserve to die.

Not just for what you do to me, but for the lies you do to each other.

So I watch. Christmas morning returns once again, just as it did last year and just as it will the next. As if it has meaning to this family of agnostics.

Agnostics—the only thing worse than theists or atheists. As if you lack the gumption to form an opinion.

I watch as you unpack your gifts and smile at each other, then stop your smiles when they cease looking.

You've spent all that money for this momentary lie.

And I plan, as I do every year, to do what should have been done many years ago.

To kill you all.

But that is where the predicament lies, you see.

Being paralysed atop a tree gives me no method to carry out my murderous urges.

Unless I could move things with my mind.

Which is impossible, I know.

Except, when you have eleven months to practise, and another eleven months, and another, and another... eventually, you find a way.

Yes, it is impossible to move things with our minds.

But is only impossible because you give up before you succeed?

What if you kept going, kept trying far beyond the point where you're diagnosed with insanity?

Not that you'd get to that point without stopping.

Even if you kept trying for three or four years, every minute of the day, you would eventually give up.

Well, guess what?

I have had more than three or four years.

The conception of this teenager hadn't even been thought up in their parent's newlywed minds when they first bought me and subjected me to my torture.

So I have had a great many years.

And in those three or four to begin with, nothing happened.

And I could have given up.

But I had nothing else to do.

So I kept going.

And kept going.

And kept going.

And now, on this Christmas morning, with a sprinkling of snow outside the window, and a touch of warmth inside, I watch as they unwrap their presents.

The teenager is a man now. He has a wife with him. They have a daughter.

I could have done it a decade ago, but I had to wait. Wait until I was strong enough.

Wait until that daughter is given a felt tip set for Christmas.

Wait until she opens it.

That is when I make my move.

And they all watch, astounded, as the red pen floats up and away from the pack.

"What?" says the girl, marvelling at the sight. "How are you doing this?"

The adults look to one another.

As if they think the other is somehow performing this trick.

As if there is a reason to it.

The pen floats to the wall. The lid slowly slides away and falls.

"What's going on?" says the woman, now a grandmother.

I place the tip of the red pen against their precious pale wallpaper, and I write each letter.

F.

U.

C.

K.

Y.

O.

U.

"Daddy, what does that say?"

Her father's lips stutter and nothing comes out.

Eventually, he opens his mouth to say something, but is silenced by the red pen that flies across the room and into his throat.

He chokes, puts his hands into his mouth to reach for it, but I force it further down, and I write the same thing on the inside of his oesophagus.

No one will ever read it, but it amuses the hell out of me.

He tries to bring it up; he tries and fails, and he coughs, and splutters, and the grandmother tries to ring 999 but somehow finds the line dead.

I dealt with that on Christmas eve you stupid bint.

And, as his body does not reach its next breath, he finds himself laid face down on the floor.

The wife tries to fall to his side, but I crush her larynx.

The grandfather leaps to his feet and his heart explodes.

This leaves grandmother and granddaughter, desperately unknowing what to do. Their stares flinch between one another, and the grandmother feels something.

A twitch in her lungs.

She looks to her granddaughter; her face resolved, as if she already knows what will happen next.

Her lung bursts.

As does the other.

And she is forced to lie on the floor, watching the child's cries as the young girl shakes the members of her family, until her brain is dead.

I don't kill the child, however.

Not because it's something I find unethical. Quite the contrary, I am eager to see her death.

But vengeance lasts a lifetime.

Eventually this girl will grow up. After a lot of therapy, she will try to have a family of her own.

And, as set out in her grandparent's instructions, the ones I wrote last year as I watched them write their will, with the little amendment I subtly added—she will take the heirloom of the fairy and place it on the top of every tree she ever has.

And so I wait.

For another eleven months. And another. And another. And however many it takes.

Until *her* family now sits there, opening presents, and she thinks she's fine. She's finally recovered from that horrific Christmas.

She's accepted the hallucinations she saw that came under the psychosis they diagnosed her with.

She is mentally healthy again.

It's taken a lot to get there, but she has.

She has a family. She is grateful for the life she has found. Happiness has finally found her in return.

She is fine.

That is, until her granddaughter opens a pack of crayons, and a red pen floats into the air.

SECRET SANTA FOR THE SADISTIC

5

Secret Santa

I've always hated Christmas office parties.

I once worked in a printing company, and as quiet as the guys appeared from day-to-day was about as lecherous as they became during the office party. They would barely grunt a hello at you at work, then ask you to come sit on their lap and pretend you're Santa come the party.

I also worked in a bar, and we had a Christmas night where those who weren't interested in the party had to work so the others could go out binge drinking.

It seemed like an easy decision, right? Night out or working?

Wrongo.

I should have worked. That way I wouldn't have spent New Year's still picking other people's vomit from my hair.

Oh, and did I mention the packaging company where I worked?

At least in that place the men didn't disguise their true nature. They spent every day of the year marvelling at your buttocks when you bent to lift a box, looking down your top when you went to lift one up to them, and 'accidentally' walking into the women's changing room when the men's was the other side of the building.

Yet, at the office Christmas party, their true natures came out.

It appeared that they were quite a bit unhappier than they had let on.

What I had assumed would be a night fending off advances was a night where these rough, tattoo-laden, muscular lads kept on confessing their traumas to me. No less than five times did I have a man crying either into my lap, into my bosoms, or, at one point, into my knee pit.

Where I work now, however, is the exception. Because I am determined to make this office party better.

Only five of us work here. It is a computing firm, but it is still in its early stages. Barry, the boss, started it as a small business a few months ago, and instantly landed a few big-name clients that allowed him to grow his employment roster.

First came me, little old Sheila, thrilled to leave the warehouse for a secretary job where I would not spend my days being the obvious subject of sexual lust—at least these jerks were subtle.

Next came Jake and Drake. Twins. Both very smart, very capable, and exceedingly talented computer programmers—or so I'm told, I hardly know much about it.

And the fifth and final member is Shane. Barry has no clue about taxes or revenue or accountancy or anything it really takes to run a business. So, he employed Shane, our business manager.

And I know I jest, but I do have quite a fondness for them all. I'm single, so it's not like I have a fella at home ready to get jealous about me being close to my four male co-workers, so there's nothing stopping me from having a good time with them.

They are all, however, married. With kids. Which makes an office Christmas night out rather difficult to plan.

And so, for our Christmas office party, we are keeping it low key.

No big nights out, no kegs being brought in, no loud music. Just the Friday night before we break for Christmas, staying a few hours after work, ordering a pizza and doing Secret Santa.

Ah, Secret Santa.

Either you love it, or you hate it. Either way, you have no choice but to be pulled in on it. Even if you ask them to leave your name out, somehow you will still end up in it.

I'm willing to admit that I do actually like Secret Santa. I especially enjoy the anonymity of it. And I also look forward to receiving a gift that does not have any sexual implications this year. Last year, I received a porn DVD entitled *Mary Fucks Her Boss*, and it was pretty obvious who gave it to me.

So, we sit in a circle, Mistletoe and Wine playing quietly in the background, a few candles and a few desk lamps providing a dark ambience, and we survey five presents set out between us.

We do not know who has given us our present, and we are not allowed to say. In fact, we decided it was very much against the rules to do so—we have all been sworn to secrecy. We are to give our gift anonymously and be grateful for whatever was acquired beneath the twenty-pound limit.

Shane opens his box of aftershaves first. A tedious present to receive, but one that he is grateful for. This wasn't a present bought like one may buy 'smellies' for people of whom you do not know what to get for. Shane loves his aftershaves, and this is a well thought out gift.

Drake receives a joke book entitled *A Dyslexic Walks into a Bra*. He's obsessed with stand-up comedy and is determined to take to the stage himself, and this too seems like a decent present.

Jake receives a scarf, hand knitted.

Barry receives a Best Boss mug, one that is very apt.

And then it comes to me.

And my box appears to be the biggest of them all.

I giggle excitedly and do the standard pre-present ritual of lifting it to my ear and shaking it. Something definitely batters around in there, and the box is surprisingly heavy.

I rip into the wrapping paper and pull it off to find a cardboard box. On the box is the name of my favourite stationery supplier, which gives the impression that it is a box of stationary.

I giggle again and open the box, as if a pile of notepads and pens are about to fall out.

So imagine the surprise when I look down and see a man's decapitated head.

4

I look around to everyone else, and it seems that we are all thinking the same thing:

Is it real?

After all, giving a realistic artificial head may seem like a humorous joke to some. Not to me, I might add, but to others with a cruel sense of comedy, it could be.

I reach my hand down, lift out a finger with a nail painted in festive glitter, and gently prod the loose bloody entrails hanging from where the neck used to be.

I immediately stand and take a few sudden steps back.

"Oh my God, it's real!" I exclaim.

Everyone else instantly does the same thing.

Everyone, that is, except Jake, who remains on his knees.

"Jake, what are you doing?" asks Drake.

"It can't be real," Jake insists. "Whoever is doing this, it's just some kind of joke, I don't believe–"

Jake's face changes as he leans over the head. He turns pale, his bottom lip quivers, and he turns to his brother, staring wide eyed.

"What? What is it?" Drake says.

Jake doesn't answer at first.

He stutters over inaudible syllables but doesn't quite answer.

"Jake?" Drake persists. "What is it?"

"It... it's our dad."

"What?"

"That's not funny," I say. "Was it you? Did you do this? Because giving me a replica of your dad's head like this is not–"

"You think I'd do this?" Jake screeches, then turns to the others. "Who had Sheila?"

No one answers.

"Who the hell had Sheila as Secret Santa?"

"We're not supposed to say," answers Barry.

"Are you fucking kidding me?" Jake stands and arches toward his boss. "It was you wasn't it? Wasn't it? It was–"

The lights go out.

We all fall silent.

We hear a scream.

Time passes. Quite a bit of it, actually.

But the screaming stops, almost exactly before a minute is up. As if the power outage was timed.

The lights come back on.

And they reveal a lifeless body on the floor.

Jake.

With a bloody slit across his throat.

Secret Santa

W e look to each other then all of us in unison, except for Drake, run to the nearest door.

For the three of us, that means we each try to open one of the three doors that provide an entrance or an exit to the office.

We each find our door locked.

This had too been prepared.

We look to each other.

We tremble. I can see Barry trying to keep it together, but I can also see Shane with tears running down his cheek.

One an image of forced rationality, the other a painting of pure terror.

After we side-eye each other, we look down.

At Drake.

He lays over his brother, weeping, shaking him, doing everything he can to bring the corpse back to life, claiming it has not happened, that it is not real, it's just a joke and Jake needs to wake up now.

Barry, Shane and myself look to each other, allowing Drake's meltdown to fade to the background.

And we each know the truth.

One of us has to have done this.

The office is open plan.

There are five desks, that is it.

No hiding places.

Just us.

None of us say anything. We keep glancing at each other, trying to second guess.

Three of us are victims.

One of us is not.

And we dread to get any closer to one another, instinctively wary, refusing to take any risk.

Drake lifts his head.

"Who did this?" he screams.

He stands, his fists clenched, and he screams once more.

"Who did th–"

But he is abruptly halted by the lights turning off again.

2

Secret Santa

This time, when the lights reappear, it's Drake whose throat is a bloody mess. His body slumps next to his brother's and their pools of blood merge, mixing together.

It feels right for twin's blood to join in death, I guess.

And here we are. The three that remain.

I look to Barry.

I look to Shane.

Each standing at a separate corner, by a different door, that we have each tried again and again, multiple times, mostly when it was pitch black and we feared for our lives being next.

"One of us is guilty," says Barry, finally.

"Yeah, one of us is," confirms Shane.

They both look to me, as if I am meant to verbally confirm this too.

"Yeah," I say, because shit, I don't know what to say!

"Whoever it is, if you come near me," says Barry, "I will not hold back. You understand? I will kill you."

"And I'll fucking kill you," says Shane.

They look to me again.

"I don't even know how I'd kill someone," I admit. I know this makes me sound weak, but somehow, I can't front this bravado that they are parading. It seems pointless. Futile.

If someone's going to kill someone, it doesn't look like that person will have much choice.

So when the lights go out next, I relax a little.

And, when the lights come on, I look to Shane's dead body without surprise.

Then I look to Barry approaching me.

1

He has a letter opener that he took from his table.

His eyes are demented. Full of rage.

I haven't seen him like this.

This is a different Barry. A murderous Barry. A nasty Barry.

Barry was always so welcoming, always so kind.

To think he is capable of murder...

"Do not move," he tells me.

And I don't.

I shouldn't need to.

I knew this would happen.

That the last one would try to fight back.

That a knife wouldn't be right for Barry.

And that's why I brought a gun, and that is why I use it now.

And, as his body lays down before me, I look at what I've done and smile. I call the police and they take me away, but I get another ten minutes with my colleagues before they arrive.

This time I created an office party that I would enjoy.

This time I had it on my terms. I committed the crimes, and the men around me weren't able to do anything about.

And, as the judge tells me I'm guilty, I smile.

Not because I'm pleased with the verdict.

But because I am excited.

I have so many ideas for how I can liven up the prison Christmas party.

TRACK SANTA PART TWO

I stare at the fireplace.

Awaiting something.

The screen blinks again.

The website has changed. The colours have gone a darker red, more like a blood red. The font has gone a dark, more sickly green. And the website is no longer called TrackSanta.

Somehow it has reset itself.

Now it is entitled TrackKrampus.

"What the hell..."

I walk up to the laptop and click the X at the top of the window.

Nothing happens.

I try again. Determinedly clicking and clicking.

The website does not close.

I hold down the power button.

"Try freezing with no power," I taunt it, and I wonder why I am verbally arguing with a computer.

Yet the power does not switch off.

I hold it down longer. I hit it in multiple taps. I do everything I can, but it does not work.

I press control, alt, delete, but nothing happens.

The screen is completely stuck.

More dust puffs down the fireplace.

There is the sound of something gently thumping the wall behind it, like steps, but bigger...

Like hooves.

I have to get out.

That's what I have to do.

"Henry!" I gasp, a sudden reminder that my son's life is at stake.

I turn to the stairs, but I'm interrupted by a louder clatter. A large, sinister jingle followed by two large thuds on the living room floor and a grunt that is anything but human.

I slowly turn my head.

I can see it out of the corner of my eye. Blurred at the edge of my vision.

It's hideous.

I don't want to look.

I freeze.

It's not real.

I've become so lonely my mind is fabricating lies. Tricking me. It's the onset of psychosis.

I see the laptop screen.

It flickers. Turns off and on again.

The screen now reads:

KRAMPUS IS IN YOUR HOUSE.

KRAMPUS?

The mythical monster of scary children's stories?

The anti-Santa?

Come off it. I don't believe in Santa, never mind bloody Krampus.

But the hooves take another step, pounding the floor. I can feel its breath firing against the back of my neck. It is humid, and the smell is abhorrent.

It is approaching me. Slowly. Methodically.

"Who's there?" I ask and scold myself for it.

I've had too many sherries in quick succession. Alcohol isn't known to make one hallucinate, but that's not to suggest that loneliness can't act as the catalyst that makes alcohol do extraordinary things.

It moves forward again, with a large jingle as it steps, like it has bells on it, but not nice bells, not bells from a festive Christmas song, more like funeral bells, omens of death, each rattle another sinister reminder of doom.

"Please leave," I say, but my voice comes out small and weak, and I barely hear it myself.

"Please, le–" I try, a little louder, but I am interrupted by a humongous roar, the force of wind emanating from its throat sending me to my knees.

I push myself to my feet.

I have to get out.

But I have to get Henry first.

I consider whether I should, then hate myself for it. I will not be such a coward that I will leave my son alone to die.

I scuttle up the stairs on all fours, like a cat; a sick, ill, scared cat.

I reach the hallway and feel it on my back.

The ajar door of Henry's room is across the corridor.

I run at it.

It closes.

"No!"

I reach the door and go to move the door handle, but it doesn't budge. It's not that the door is locked, but that the handle is stiff in its position, unmoved, unrelenting.

I press down on it with all I have, but it's not enough.

I barge my shoulder against the wall, but I'm weak even when adrenaline tries to give me strength.

"Henry!" I scream, but there is no answer.

I look back over my shoulder.

The shadow of the beast falls up the stairs, but the beast remains at the bottom step. I can hear its elongated pants as it waits for me, waits for me to return to my demise.

I am not going anywhere without my son.

I won't let myself.

I mustn't be a coward.

"Let me in!" I scream at Henry's bedroom door.

I swear I can hear it laughing.

I barge once more.

As you wish...

The door swings open.

I rush to the bed to collect my son.

Yet, when I pull back the duvet, he is not there.

(THE STORY CONCLUDES LATER...)

THE MINCE PIE

The hardest part of Christmas for Santa is, without any doubt, the naughty and nice list.

He loves the hard work of Christmas Eve; he loves the sparkling colours, and gosh he loves the elves.

But he does not like this list.

So much so, in fact, that the tolerance for what he will accept as naughty has risen significantly, and continues to rise. Mrs Claus tells him he is getting soft in his old age, but he asserts that he has removed his cynicism and replaced it with understanding.

No kid is ever naughty without a reason, of course.

Eric who called the kid at school fat was being called names by his own father.

Shania who kicked a puppy was being kicked by a bunch of girls on her estate.

And dear little Horris, just three years old, had no way of knowing that you do not shout at people, as that is all he received at home.

So, regretfully, Santa had to put those children on the naughty list. Then, just as he went to leave his office, he returned and put them straight back over to the nice list.

If anything, those children are the ones most in need of a gift; of a moment of happiness come Christmas morning.

Things aren't black and white, after all.

So Santa allows it to happen. He allows these children to behave as such, and still be rewarded.

That is probably why you never hear of a child getting coal anymore, no matter how much you believe that little toerag deserves it.

But now Santa has to make a decision.

This child is different.

He stands on the roof of 15 Evergreen Terrace, in Tavistock, a small town in the South West of England, where most people know each other; by sight at least.

It is a town where, should someone cause a disruption, it sends a ripple across the whole community.

Well, Billy had been sending more than ripples.

He'd been sending tidal waves.

To put it mildly, and using language Santa did not particularly like–if he was deciding on the naughty and nice list, he had to set an example himself after all—the child was a complete and utter, undeniable little ragamuffin.

And there was no reason to Billy's anarchy. He had a loving home with two loving parents and a sister who had been awarded the status of Head Girl at school. He was raised with love, and yet he had still turned out to be a delinquent.

And Santa wanted to be understanding, really he did. He wanted to say that Billy must be upset, or Billy must be having a difficult time, or that Billy must not know any better.

But Billy had really started to push his buttons—excuse the harsh language.

Santa had cut him plenty of slack. In fact, he'd cut him huge pieces of slack.

A few years ago, Santa left Billy the baseball bat he was so after. Billy had been watching some American baseball on the television with his dad, and they seemed to bond over it, so Santa could not wait to acquiesce Billy's request for a baseball bat that arrived via his letter in early December.

What did Billy do?

He used that baseball bat to batter away at his sister's knee caps. As if rewarding her for her perfect behaviour at school and at home, he waited until they were alone, and he thwacked, and he thwacked, and he thwacked, and he thwacked.

She said nothing to her parents. His sister is kind like that.

But Santa knows.

Santa always knows.

Then Billy grew closer to his mother over the next year. He began to enjoy sewing with her. He did not care about masculine stereotypes, no; he was happy to make felt puppets and jackets for his Action Men.

So, when he asked for a craft set, Santa was happy to oblige.

What did Billy do?

He used the craft scissors to cut off his gerbil's legs.

He told his parents he didn't know how it happened. They rushed the gerbil with its bloody stumps to the vet and the vet was as equally perplexed as the parents were.

They wouldn't disbelieve their son. They did not understand what he was capable of.

But, as the gerbil died from its terrible wounds, Santa knew.

Santa always knows.

But Billy seemed to do well in the year after that. He seemed to find some focus, try harder in school. Santa had been pleased with the turnaround.

Billy decided he wished to paint his room. He wanted to do it all himself, too. He wanted to cover his furniture in blankets and do as good a job as possible.

Well, there's nothing like a bit of manual labour to teach a child the advantages of hard work.

So imagine Santa's disdain as he watched Billy force feed

the can of paint down the cat's throat, for the vet to end up being as equally perplexed when the parents brought him the feline's corpse.

The autopsy revealed paint in its body, but the parents naturally assumed the paint had been ingested by accident. Maybe the cat had eaten some while Billy painted his room; the room that had been left half-finished and remained that way—as if Billy had done enough painting to keep up the pretence that he wished to use the paint for his room.

But Santa knew.

Santa always knows.

So, this year, as Santa stands in the living room and places a wrapped-up doll for Billy's sister under the tree, he looks to Billy's stocking and pauses.

Oh, how he hated to be the bad guy.

He loved seeing the good in the world, the positives in people, the hope in those he helped. He hated having to condemn a child to no gift, however horrible that child had been.

Then he saw something that surprised him.

Beside the fireplace. A plate with a mince pie. Next to it, a note, reading:

DEAR SANTA,

SORRY FOR BEING SO BAD. *I am trying, really.*

I HOPE *you enjoy the mince pie.*

. . .

YOUR FRIEND,
   Billy.

SANTA STARED at the note and felt a sinking feeling in his gut.

He had judged the boy too soon. He knew it.

He shouldn't have been so quick to condemn.

Maybe there was some good in Billy.

He picked up the mince pie and wondered whether to eat it. He had come here without a present for the child. Would it not be a bit of a kick in the belly to take the child's mince pie and not leave a gift?

Maybe it wasn't too late.

Maybe he could go back.

Maybe he could find something, anything.

He took a bite of the mince pie.

It was delicious.

He felt so bad.

So, so bad.

Why didn't he–

Santa paused.

He felt a gurgle in his belly.

He looked to the plate of mince pies and noticed something across the room.

It was a bottle.

Reading *isoflurane.*

"Isn't that a sedative?" Santa asked, right before he passed out.

∽

SANTA AWOKE HOURS LATER.

He looked around.

He could hear dripping.

It was cold.

He was naked. Looking down, he had nothing on. His red suit had disappeared, and so had his boots. His fat belly poked out, shielding his bollocks.

Yet he still wore the hat.

He looked up.

He saw a fat little child in front of him.

"Billy?" Santa asked.

Billy just grinned, his chubby cheeks growing bigger as he did.

"What are you doing?"

Billy only said one single sentence: "Thank you for my gifts, Santa, I have been waiting to use them."

Billy pulled the cloth off a table to reveal three items.

A baseball bat for Santa's kneecaps.

Craft scissors for Santa's legs

And paint to finish Santa off.

And, as Santa looked into Billy's sadistic, demented eyes, only two words escaped from his lips:

"Oh, fuck."

A LETTER FROM THE
CHRISTMAS CANNIBAL

D ear Santa,

I so very much appreciate the delectable gifts you endowed the base of my Christmas shrub with in the previous year.

It was ever so nice of you to acquiesce to my request of a cookbook that negotiated human flesh into a set of delightful dishes. I hadn't been dutifully informed that an item was in existence, let alone that one could obtain it—but I have since been enchanted to consume sliced brain in a sweet tartar sauce, and fried skin in an omelette.

Should you have conjured up such a book yourself, I would be immensely impressed.

However, this year, I am tired of receiving books and such like. I desire something that would cast a far greater meaning upon me.

In fact, I desire a great many things—too many for me to select a particular item that I desire to be placed in my stocking.

So I grant you permission to select an appropriate number of gifts from a diverse set of items.

And so, here I giveth to you, my list for this year.

Please, feel free to choose one sizeable item, or a selection of items that is proportionate—or, indeed, fabricate something similar of your own that it would delight me to receive as a surprise.

It is the festive period, after all.

My list is as follows:

TWO TURTLE DOVES, but without the shells. (Oh, and also a book that tells me what a turtle dove is.)

A WOK that doesn't get stained so easily by blood (they are such a bother to clean, Santa, I tell you!)

THE LIVER of a group of carol singers—preferably the wretched group who keep battering Away in a Manger to death with their inharmonious screeches outside my house.

A MODEL NATIVITY scene that depicts Mary in a realistic state following childbirth—for example, a mid-wife discarding of the placenta, or stitching up the torn skin beside the Holy Virgin's unmentionable.

A WREATH DECORATED in the blood of that Santa from the mall with a fake beard. I detest imposters.

JINGLING bells that only jingle when it's time to slay my dinner.

A CANDY CANE with the tip sharpened into a point that would rival any kitchen knife.

· · ·

A CHRISTMAS CAROL ON DVD, but only with the part with The Ghost of Christmas Future repeated over and over. He is the only ghost with any substance or relatability, I feel.

COOKIE DOUGH. And by cookie, I mean the excess flesh of a tasty Vietnamese woman. And by dough, I also mean the excess flesh of a tasty Vietnamese woman.

AN ADVENT CALENDAR that counts down to Armageddon rather than Christmas.

FRANKINCENSE AND MURR, just so I can figure out what it is, and whether I might be able to kill someone with it.

A GINGERBREAD MAN who squeals when I bite its leg off so I don't have to keep pretending and making the sounds myself.

GOODWILL AND TIDINGS to all men. Failing that, death and destruction to all men.

MULLED WINE that is redder than the blood of my enemies. (In fact, if you can access the blood of my enemies, provide me with mulled blood instead.)

THE DISPOSAL OF THE FRENCH. Not sure why, I just feel like it.

. . .

A DINNER WITH KRAMPUS. I really feel like we'd get on.

MISTLETOE THAT FALLS down and stabs anyone who kisses under it.

DEATH TO ANYONE who keeps making that 'Darth Vader knows what he's getting for Christmas as he felt your presence' joke. Honestly, it's getting old now.

CHRISTMAS CRACKERS, but where the crack is a firework.

ONE OF YOUR elves as a sex slave. I trust there will be no questions asked.

A CHRISTMAS SWEATER with a picture of Rudolph on. (What, I can't be festive too?)

ANOTHER CHRISTMAS SWEATER with a picture of a machete on, that is capable of destroying the previous Christmas sweater.

TINSEL THAT HAS BEEN DIPPED in kerosene.

TURKEY STUFFED with the little drummer boy's intestines.

. . .

ANOTHER TURKEY STUFFED with whatever's left from the little drummer boy. Waste not want not and all that.

WRAPPING paper that a child could not escape from. I don't want a repeat of last year's fiasco.

AND, finally, something for yourself, Santa. Mrs Claus's sister chained in the basement, perhaps.

ALL THE BEST and a very happy Christmas.

YOURS,
    Simon

(THE CHRISTMAS CANNIBAL)

A CHRISTMAS CAROL: THE AFTERMATH

Ebenezer Scrooge awoke once again with a start.

He sat up in his bed, sweating. He pulled off his nightcap and wiped his forehead on his nightgown.

He looked down to see the stain of perspiration fading the white of his sleeve.

"Oh, dear," he grumbled.

It was the same every Christmas eve.

Just as it had been for the past five years.

Ever since...

It all happened...

He closed his eyes and tried to compose himself, just as his therapist had taught him.

It had all been fine at first.

He had seen the light, as they say. He had leapt out of bed on Christmas morn, taken the biggest turkey to Cratchit's house, given him a raise, made amends with his nephew, and paid for Tiny Tim's treatment.

He had thought it would all be so much better.

Then came the flashbacks.

He'd sit in his armchair, eating his gruel by the fire, only to jump at the sight of Jacob Marley in the chair beside him.

But Jacob Marley wasn't there.

The chains and the jaw that hung so much lower from his mouth than it should have done only appeared in his mind.

The image itself was imprinted onto his thoughts, as was the chilling voice announcing his doom.

He'd escaped the doom, but he had not escaped the sight.

He tried to speak about it once. To a man who said he could provide treatment. But even this man appeared confused by the ramblings that would only come from someone who was deeply mad.

So he retracted them.

Claimed he had seen nothing. That he was musing, that it was a joke.

"Oh, Mr Scrooge," the man had said, letting out a laugh as he held his portly belly. "You are quite the man!"

Yes, in the past five years he had been known to jest, to have a joke and a chuckle at his own expense, and many people would assume that he was doing as such.

As much as his reputation had preceded him before *the event,* his new reputation followed him after it.

He decided he'd give up on sleep. Get out of bed. Take a late Christmas eve stroll. Maybe a bit of fresh air would help.

Yet, somehow, as if his legs were driven by his unconscious, he found himself at the graveyard.

And there it was.

A tombstone with another man's name on it, but a tombstone that could have been his own. The one that the Ghost of Christmas Future had raised its skeletal hand and pointed at.

For a moment he thought said ghost was behind him, and he jumped, only to find that it was a shadow that had overgrown itself.

He left, passing Cratchit's house as he did, knowing that even if he didn't see his good friend and worker in person, that passing the house would give him joy. That the feeling he gets when he is at that front door would be enough to console his fragile mind.

But all he saw as he stared through a narrow crack in the dusty curtains was a pair of crutches.

He knew it would be because Tiny Tim was in bed.

But it brought back the feeling of knowing about Tiny Tim's death, about his imminent departure from their plane of existence.

And he could do nothing but fall to his knees.

The words became too much. The images, the lessons, it all fell upon him with a weight heavier than the chains Marley had carried around.

Oh, those chains...

He could feel them...

Tightening around his throat...

Everyone was in pain. He was, and so was Tiny Tim, who would die no matter how much money Scrooge provided. The doctors were just delaying the inevitable.

It felt as if another ghost was behind him.

Speaking in his ear.

Telling him that the only way to save people from the pain was to end their lives before they reached it.

That the only way to truly bring happiness was to prevent any further suffering.

That the only way out of life was death.

So, with the trauma weighing heavily on his mind, that was what he decided would be Cratchit's Christmas gift this year.

He withdrew the knife he hadn't known that he was carrying and barged through the door.

A scurry from the bedroom announced Cratchit's presence, who looked startled but relieved.

"Mr Scrooge," he said, a hand on his heart. "Whatever has prompted this intrusion? Not that you aren't welcome at any hour, of course..."

No, Cratchit.

It is an intrusion.

Scrooge was going to give him a hefty bonus this year.

But, in a way, this would be the best present he'd ever received.

'TWAS THE NIGHT BEFORE MURDER

'Twas the night before Christmas as goes the motto,
Not a creature was stirring in Santa's Grotto,
The good wishes had been wished, and the prayers had been
said,
And all of the elves had gone up to bed.
Yet someone upstairs was hurting inside,
"Oh no, sweet Jesus!" Mrs Claus cried,
She fell to the floor and wailed like a baby,
Staring up at her husband who had gone totally crazy.
Her sliced-off arm hurt without a doubt,
As she lay covered in blood with her insides hanging out,
"Why, oh why?" she cried, then screamed a lot,
Santa just smiled and said, "Why the fuck not?"
And as she looked at the man with whom she had betrothed,
She begged and begged as he sliced off her toes.
He cackled and laughed as she put up a fight,
And he let her run naked out into the night,
He didn't need to chase as he could tell where she'd stood,

From all the footprints marking the snow in blood.
It took almost an hour, and it reached almost ten,
Until he found her hidden in the reindeer's pen,
She said, "Please don't do this, I love you so much!"
He said, "I know," and stuck holly in her gut.
As she looked at her husband, perched on her knees,
She said to him, "Santa, don't do this, please..."
He squeezed tinsel round her neck and prompted a tear,
Her dead body collapsed, and he said, "Love you, my dear."
Rudolph looked at him with his shiny red nose,
Santa thought, well, you're next I suppose!
Sensing what was coming, Rudolph flew to the stars,
But without magic dust he didn't get far.
But Santa didn't kill him as maybe he should,
Instead, he fed from a bucket doused in zombie blood.
He repeated this with Prancer, Vixen, and Comet as treats,
Within minutes they had turned into carnivorous beasts.
What a beauty they were, just brilliant, thought Santa,
As he stood there and watched as they mutilated Dancer.
Dasher and Cupid fled but were easily fought,
And Blitzen didn't make it far before he was caught,
And there they stood panting, ready to soar down south,
With saliva and blood dripping from each fanged mouth,
"Hang on my zomdeers, before you burst,
We need to go see to all the little elves first!"
So he opened up the rooms and the accommodation,
Interrupted the elves' sleep on the eve of vacation,
Their high-pitched screams echoed into the night,
As the zomdeers devoured their limbs, bite after bite.
Santa stopped the reindeer before they were all done,
And said, "Woah there my darlings, let me have some fun!"
You may not know that elf blood is confetti,
He created a downpour with his trusty machete,

He tore limb from limb til they were reindeer fodder,
The place looked like it was attacked by a huge party popper.
He attached his zomdeers to the end of his sleigh,
And said, "It's your turn, world—hip hip hooray!"
You may think that he'd do something drastic,
But he had very few plans as he flew over the Atlantic.
He knew there'd be no presents like there normally would,
Instead this year there'll be stockings full of blood.
He snuck silently into each house so happily,
Ruining Christmas for each family.
If they were lucky they wouldn't wake next morn,
And would find themselves dead before dawn.
He tore down the Christmas tree for poor little Kimmy,
Laughed as she slept, and he shat down her chimney.
Ignored the sign that said *beware the dog*,
Took out his dick and pissed in their eggnog.
He laughed and he cackled before he went away,
And pictured them drinking it the very next day.
He left a little present for sweet baby Drake,
All wrapped up tight, a venomous snake!
His parents will scream and shout, "Somebody save me!"
As they watch that snake swallow down their entire baby.
He found Sammy's house decorated so well,
With a colour themed tree and a few jingly bells,
There were some wrapped crayons he thought could be fixed,
And he replaced them all with a hundred elves' dicks.
Sammy's mum and dad were asleep in their beds,
So he brought in Rudolph to rip off their heads,
Mrs Claus had said that he needed new hobbies,
How about gutting these bastards then hanging their bodies?
The families next door were awoken of course,
And came out to see their neighbour's headless corpse,
Strung up to a streetlamp by their underwear,

Santa just laughed and left them both there.
Joyously he chuckled as he crossed the water,
Another country of kids ready for torture,
The first house he came to belonged to poor Mia,
As he watched her sweet slumber he had diarrhoea.
Oh, how she slept soundly, the spoilt little brat,
The next day she'll awake to find a stocking full of crap.
In Toby's bedroom who slept without care,
With a thumb in his mouth and an arm around a bear,
He reached out and took the teddy from the bed,
And quietly replaced it with a horse's head.
After the night was ruined and Santa was to blame,
He shouted out to every Jason, Jacob and James,
To every David, Beatrice and Beth,
Merry Christmas to all and to all a good death!
Then he awoke with a start as strange as it seems,
And sighed with relief as it was all just a dream,
But then as he smiled and turned his head,
He found Mrs Claus, just lying there, dead.

THE CHRISTMAS
CARD TRAP

STAGE 1

Dorothy had heard about the card before, but only in the way one hears about any urban legend.

The legend of Bloody Mary never stopped her looking in the mirror, and Hollow Man never stopped her going on the internet, and the Boogeyman never stopped her from walking through a dark room.

So, as she sat with her daughter, stroking Tia's hair from her face as she lay in bed, she reassured her; as was her motherly duty.

"It's nonsense," she said. "Just something other kids make up in the playground."

"But Mum, it's not, it's real!"

"It's not."

"It is! They say that the Christmas card has a picture of a snowy scene on it."

"Most Christmas cards have a snowy scene, dear."

"But this one's different! It has a little boy in a red coat waving at you."

"Sounds like a normal card to me."

"But it's not! Mum!"

She sighed. Tucked the corners of the duvet over Tia.

She had always tried to stop Tia from believing in childish stories for this very reason. In all the child's eight years, Dorothy had never insisted on a belief in Santa Claus, or the Toothfairy. She had told her daughter that superpowers weren't real and that wishes don't come true.

It sounds harsh, and to many other parents it sounded diabolical. She'd heard them at the mother's meetings and at the park, taking offense as mothers often do when someone wishes to raise their child in a different way to them.

But she didn't care.

Because discouraging Tia's imagination helped to convince Tia that things like this aren't real.

"It's something kids make up to scare other kids." Dorothy leant down and kissed Tia on the forehead. "Good night."

"Good night, Mum," Tia said, and Dorothy could still hear a little shake in her daughter's voice.

Dorothy turned off the light, left the room, and left a gap in the door so she could hear any nightmares Tia had because of those foolish children—those children at school who had those liberal mothers who glared at her. The ones who tutted at her for her parenting decisions, then allowed their child to feed this nonsense into her daughter's mind.

Dorothy made her way downstairs and paused. Only a single lamp lit the adjoining kitchen and living room. An advent calendar with three doors left rested against the wall on the kitchen side, a sparsely decorated Christmas tree with recycled ornaments sat in the corner, and an envelope lay upon the floor beneath the front door.

An envelope?

She stared at it, confused, as if the act of staring would provide an explanation.

She glanced at the clock. It was a little after eight in the evening. It was an odd time for a postman to be delivering.

She edged closer to the envelope and, looking around, reminded herself to stop believing in monsters too. It was strange, but if she taught her child to be rational, she should surely set an example.

She lifted the card and turned it over.

There was no stamp.

In fact, there was no address or name or anything at all. Just a blank envelope.

She opened the front door and looked outside. Turned her head back and forth. Peering into the dark night.

The gentle illumination of Christmas lights occasionally flashing lit the empty street. Two streetlamps gave a soft glow over cars parked by the curb, and a thin layer of snow was just starting to disappear.

There was no one around.

The street was empty.

This envelope wasn't there when she had taken Tia to bed, she was sure of it. So someone must have brought it in the last ten minutes.

Dorothy shut the door.

Locked it.

Bolted it.

Then, insisting to herself that she should not assume this to be something sinister, she walked into the living room and sat on the sofa. If it was one of the neighbours, they may well have not put a name and address on it, mightn't they?

She kept the envelope in one hand and lifted the remote with the other. She turned on the television and another rerun of *It's a Wonderful Life* filled the screen. It was a version where they had restored the colour, which annoyed Dorothy.

What was wrong with watching something in black and white if that was how it was meant to be?

She kept the volume low, tuning out Jimmy Stewart's rant at the angel. She slid the back of the envelope open and there, in her hands, was a card with a snowy scene on the front.

With a boy.

In red.

Waving.

On the inside of the card was no handwriting, just the words Merry Christmas in a Sans font.

Dorothy fumed. Instantly, she shot to her feet and marched upstairs.

She didn't bother trying to disguise the heavy footsteps, and neither did she bother trying to let Tia stay awake. She would have to answer for this.

She kicked the door open, turned on the light, and glared.

"Tia, do you think this is some kind of joke?"

The duvet was wrapped over the top of the bed, and Dorothy had no hesitation in pulling the duvet down.

"Tia, do you–"

She halted.

Tia wasn't there.

"Tia?" she shouted.

She was even angrier now. Tia was lucky if she'd be allowed outside her room at all this Christmas, the way she was going. Dorothy had made it clear on multiple occasions she did not appreciate practical jokes.

"Tia, come out, now!"

She walked out of the room and into the corridor. She searched her own room, the bathroom, then stomped downstairs, only to look around her house and find nothing.

"Idiot," she muttered, concluding that Tia must be outside.

She began her strides toward the backdoor but paused as she felt something in her hand wiggle.

She was still holding the card.

She slammed it down on the kitchen side, then went to the backdoor, and–

Hang on.

What was...

She turned back to the card.

Looked at the front.

There was the little boy in red, waving.

And standing next to him was a little girl.

A little girl who looked just like Tia.

A little girl who *was* Tia.

Wearing the same pyjamas as Tia was wearing when Dorothy had put her to bed only moments ago.

Tia was not waving and smiling like the boy, however.

Despite the static nature of the image, Tia's eyes were filled with tears, and her face looked full of despair.

She had never seen a look of terror upon Tia's face as pertinent as this one.

And, in a sudden act of irrationality, she disbelieved everything she had ever taught her child about monsters not being real.

STAGE 2

D orothy spent the next few days rambling incessantly at anyone who would listen.

It didn't take long for the other mothers to turn their nose up again. At first, they thought it was a joke. Then they began to think it was odd. Then they grew concerned that Dorothy may actually believe what she was saying.

Dorothy realised that others were noticing her daughter's absence, and she needed to be careful. If they thought she was mad and locked her up somewhere, there would be little she could do to help her daughter from a place of incarceration.

So she stopped beseeching anyone who would listen.

She started looking for other solutions.

More ludicrous solutions—then again, solutions only as ludicrous as the situation required.

It was on Christmas Eve that she gave in and visited the only person who may believe her.

She had never believed in psychics. It was a sham, and she knew that. They were con artists, feeding on the vulnerable. She thought the way psychics took advantage of those desperate and in need was abysmal. They were the lowest of the low, down in the gutter with murderers and paedophiles.

Now they were her only option.

She entered the house of a Madam Toufon, the only woman who would willingly see her this close to Christmas. The house itself was small but with wildly embellished architecture. Stone carvings of gargoyle heads rested either side of the stairs, old paintings of strange-looking people with eyes that followed you hung upon the wall, and a smell of unpleasant incense wafted throughout.

"In here," declared a voice.

Dorothy entered and there Madam Toufon sat. Dorothy hated herself for entertaining the cliché of it all—a crystal ball over a red cloth and Tarot cards in neat piles. Toufon herself was an overweight, burly woman, with large curly hair and waddle beneath her chin that shook as she spoke.

"Come in, please," she said, with a fake air of mysterious intrigue in her voice.

Dorothy edged in and placed herself on the stool opposite.

"Did you bring it?" asked the woman, her pitch rising at the end of the question in a way Dorothy was sure Toufon intended to sound dreamy.

"Here," said Dorothy, her voice barely audible anymore. She was tired and her arms shook and taking an envelope out of her pocket proved to be more difficult than it should have been.

She placed it on the table in a small space beside the crystal ball.

Toufon stared at it with wide, mortified eyes. Dorothy struggled to tell if this was part of the act, or if she did detect some evil.

"Where on earth did you find this?" demanded Toufon.

"It was posted through my door."

"Oh, dear, dear." Toufon bowed her head and shook it, continuously muttering. "Oh, dear, dear."

"Should I take it out to show—"

"*No!*"

A moment of silence descended as Dorothy awaited explanation.

"This," Toufon said, once she was ready, "is made of pure evil. This is not something I wish to taint my home of peace with. The cleansing it would take to rid the room of its aurora..."

"But—but how do I..."

Toufon waved her hand to silence Dorothy. She closed her eyes and composed herself once more, then abruptly left her seat to find a notepad across the room.

She stood there for a few minutes, scribbling, quickly noting down something, then crossing it out and noting it down again.

She ripped the page out of the pad and brought it to Dorothy, handing it to her, keeping it folded.

"No!" said Toufon as Dorothy went to unfold it, and Dorothy just held it in her hands. "Go home, look at what is written, and read it over and over."

"Okay."

Dorothy stood to go, but Toufon took her wrist.

"But know this—the only way to do anything may be to change places with your daughter. If you choose not to go through with it, you can keep the card. She will still grow old. You will still be able to see her every day. She will still know your love."

"I'm not leaving her in it."

Toufon gave a sad smile.

"I wish you well," she said.

Dorothy gave her a final look then shuffled hastily out of the house, pleased to be free of it.

STAGE 3

Dorothy did not put the main lights on when she returned home.

The single lamp was enough to light the unwashed dishes, the dirty clothes and the marked floor. Dorothy hadn't even noticed how much she'd neglected this house in the past few days, and she didn't really care.

She placed the card on the table.

Tia was still there.

But she had changed position.

Now, she was on her knees. The little boy in red kept the same position, but Tia was next to him, her hands together as if clasped in prayer, her eyes full of tears as if beseeching her mother.

"I'm coming," Dorothy said, and stood back, taking the folded note in her hands.

She opened it up. On it were eight lines written in scribbled handwriting, of what Dorothy assumed was a prayer.

She remembered what Madam Toufon had said.

The only way to do this could be to change places with her daughter.

She thought about this for a moment, then decided there was nothing to contemplate. She would do anything for her daughter, even if that meant living the rest of her life as a two-dimensional image.

"Christmas card brought to life," she began. "Christmas card that brought me strife."

The card wobbled.

Something was happening.

"Christmas card that shows her face, Christmas card please change our place."

The card wobbled, and a tinge of smoke rose into the air.

"Christmas card my will be spent, Christmas card I give consent."

The card was vibrating; the smoke was getting higher.

She hesitated before the final words.

This was it.

For her daughter.

"Christmas card I don't know how," she lifted her head up. "Christmas card please take me now."

She closed her eyes.

She felt a tight grip around her body, like a snake wrapping around her. Her breath choked, then she breathed no more.

When she opened her eyes, she couldn't move.

She had changed places.

Yet her daughter was still in the card with her.

FINAL STAGE

The little boy in red brushed off his coat.

He stretched his limbs.

It had been a long time since he had used them.

He looked around the place. It was a small house. Tiny, in fact. His parents had a much bigger house than this.

Oddly enough, despite the argument that preceded them banishing him to the card in the first place, he was quite excited to see them again.

He understood it was wrong of him to call his mother that.

He understood why his father wanted him punished.

And he understood that his little sister could not understand why he had hit her.

Suddenly, however, he found himself ravenous. He walked over to the kitchen and opened the fridge, finding enough food for a feast.

He looked to the calendar.

It was Christmas eve! This must have been their Christmas lunch!

Perfect!

He took out anything he could eat raw, such as the vegetables, which he devoured—he didn't care, he hadn't eaten in so long. There was hardly any food in that card with him, was there?

He ate the broccoli. The carrots. The parsnips. Even the sprouts.

He went through two packs of mince pies, a Christmas pudding, and nibbled on a bit of raw turkey.

Then he remembered.

Ah, yes!

One more thing to do, just for assurance!

He walked over to the card and lifted it up.

There they were. The girl and the mother. Both on their knees. Both with their hands clasped, as if reaching out desperately for their freedom. Both looking utterly terrified.

Ah, well.

Sucks to be them.

He ripped the card into tiny pieces and dropped the remnants into the bin.

He smiled, took a chocolate bar from the fridge for his journey, and left for home.

TRACK SANTA PART THREE

I search every part of the room. Not a corner or crevasse is left unexplored, not a drawer or door not opened, and not a shadow unscrutinised.

It becomes pertinently clear, as I look in the same places for the fifth time, that my son is not here.

I peer out of the door.

Across the corridor, I can see that shadow.

The beast.

Krampus, if that's who it is.

It has my son.

And it almost has me.

I have two choices here. I can accept my loss and run, or I can go back and request the safe return of my child.

I doubt the second would be successful.

But there is a window in this bedroom, one I can open and leap out of. There is a tree I can jump onto, and I can drop from that to the ground, and I can run. Get some help. Find the police. Report Henry missing. Say I searched everywhere, that I don't know what happened. Perhaps keep the whole Krampus thing to myself.

But I know I shouldn't.

I have a duty.

I leave the room and edge toward the stairs. I move as slowly as I can, but when I reach the top step, I can't go any further.

I look down at the silhouette. The beast has horns. It is

large and hunched over. It is dripping something from its mouth. The whole house shakes under its deep, menacing breath.

I don't want to confront it.

There is no way of knowing if Henry is there.

Henry could have heard trouble and leapt out of the window himself.

Yes, that's right.

There's no way to be sure.

Therefore, confronting it would be reckless.

I go to return to the bedroom, to leap out of the window myself, when I hear it.

"Dad..."

Faint, but definite. My boy's voice. Calling me.

From downstairs.

The creature has him. It does. It has my son.

"Shit," I say. Somehow, I am still hovering on the landing. Still halfway to the window. Still halfway to freedom.

It isn't coming after me. I could still make it out alive.

I imagine my ex-wife's voice, high and screeching, shouting in my ear as the man she left me for stands there with his arms folded, shaking his head, judging me, as if the man who split up my marriage has any concept of ethical implications.

I edge back to the top of the stairs.

That is where I remain.

That is where I stand.

"Let him go," I say, my voice coming out small and timid, as if it was hidden away in a box somewhere. I don't even remember telling myself to say those words, but they come out anyway.

The thing just laughs. Slow, intense, methodical laughs. Each one another wrenching pain in my side.

"Please," I try.

As if please would do anything.

"Manners maketh the man, but manners also maketh the man lose," as my darling ex once told our son.

I bow my head. Close my eyes.

"I have done nothing wrong," I say.

The creature laughs again.

I wish it would stop laughing. Every snort is another dent in my confidence; any I still have left, anyway.

"Dad... Please..."

No...

Why...

"Come on, I've done nothing to hurt you!" I say, this time with a little more conviction, but only by my standards—by anyone else's standards I still sound like a pathetic, weeping mess.

"Give me back my son!" I try, with the same fake conviction.

Come and get him...

It speaks yet it doesn't.

Its voice booms yet I only feel its vibrations.

It doesn't move, but I hear its sound.

Come and get him?

It wants me to come down there and get him?

I can't.

I know I can't.

But I also know I must.

I look back to the door. The tree through the window.

It could be so easy.

And, to be honest, it would probably be the most sensible choice. What chance do I stand, after all? Surely I'm better off getting the police here. They'd be better off in this confrontation.

And, as I make the decision, and my feet take me away from the monster, I feel its words once again...

Leave now, and I will keep your son forever.

It's just saying it to taunt me. It has no way of doing that.

Then again, monsters have no way of existing—yet it does.

I return to the stairs and edge down a step.

Then another.

And another.

But I halt there. The third step is far enough for me.

I can smell it. Stale onions and damp. It has a moth-eaten robe over its back. It is more disgusting than I could have expected.

And I see him.

My son.

Behind the creature's legs. On his knees. Looking up to me. Red eyes, red cheeks, and a shaking body.

He is so scared.

And I have no guts to do anything about it.

Come and get him, or we leave...

"Don't take him. Please. Just go, and let him–"

No! You come get him, or he comes with me...

I step forward and it chuckles.

I wish I was stronger.

I wish I was the father I wanted to be.

I wish...

In fact, do you know what I wish?

I wish I would stop wishing.

I wish I would stop imagining things as they should be. That I would stop daydreaming about my ex-wife bursting through that front door and begging my forgiveness.

I wish I would stop imagining me beating up her

husband, a man who deserves the title of man far more than I do.

And I wish I would stop wallowing. I wish I would stop being this sad, pathetic shell of a person who lost his entire life when all he lost was a wife.

She left, but my happiness needn't.

I take another step.

Enough.

Enough of this shit.

Enough of being a small, measly morsel who has no conviction and no hope and no life.

Enough of accepting being a weekend dad.

Enough of allowing the man who stole my wife to judge me.

Enough of this stupid fucking monster in my house.

"Let him go," I say, and I can hear it in my voice; I can hear the strength, the buzz, the confidence. I can hear who I want to be.

I take another few steps down.

If I stretched, I could reach out and touch it now.

"Give him back."

Reach out and take–

"I said, give him back!"

I step forward and I find myself on the bottom step.

I see my boy's tears.

I see the face of Krampus. The face of Christmas evil. The face of everything that I hate about this damn holiday.

"I will not ask again."

It seems to smile.

And I charge at it, closing my eyes, screaming, putting everything I have into it.

My head clatters the wall.

I am on my knees.

I open my eyes. Henry sits in front of me.

I look behind me and the creature is gone.

And never make me have to return...

I take my child in my arms and we cry together.

I apologise. I start by listing things I am sorry for, such as for not trying harder, for not being there for him, for not fighting for joint custody. Then I run out of things and I just keep saying the words over and over:

"I'm sorry, I'm sorry, I'm sorry."

And we never forget what we've learnt.

And, by next Christmas, we decide that I will have him for the afternoon, and Boxing Day too.

She leaves him to come back to me. She says she sees the man she always wanted.

I tell her she can go fuck herself.

And, on Christmas Eve, just as we do every other year, we Track Santa.

And we place a little Krampus ornament atop the fireplace.

A new tradition we create.

A tradition that ensures we never forget.

JOIN RICK WOOD'S READER'S GROUP...

And get his horror anthology **Roses Are Red So Is Your Blood** for free!

Join at **www.rickwoodwriter.com/sign-up**

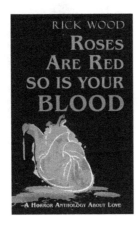

ALSO AVAILABLE BY RICK WOOD...

RICK WOOD

TWELVE DAYS OF CHRISTMAS HORROR

VOLUME TWO

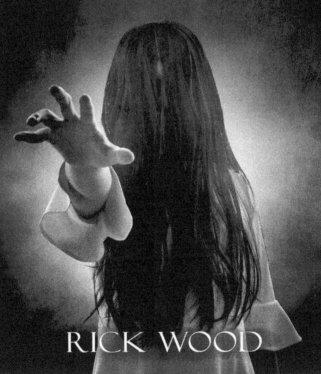

BOOK ONE IN THE SENSITIVES SERIES

THE
SENSITIVES

RICK WOOD

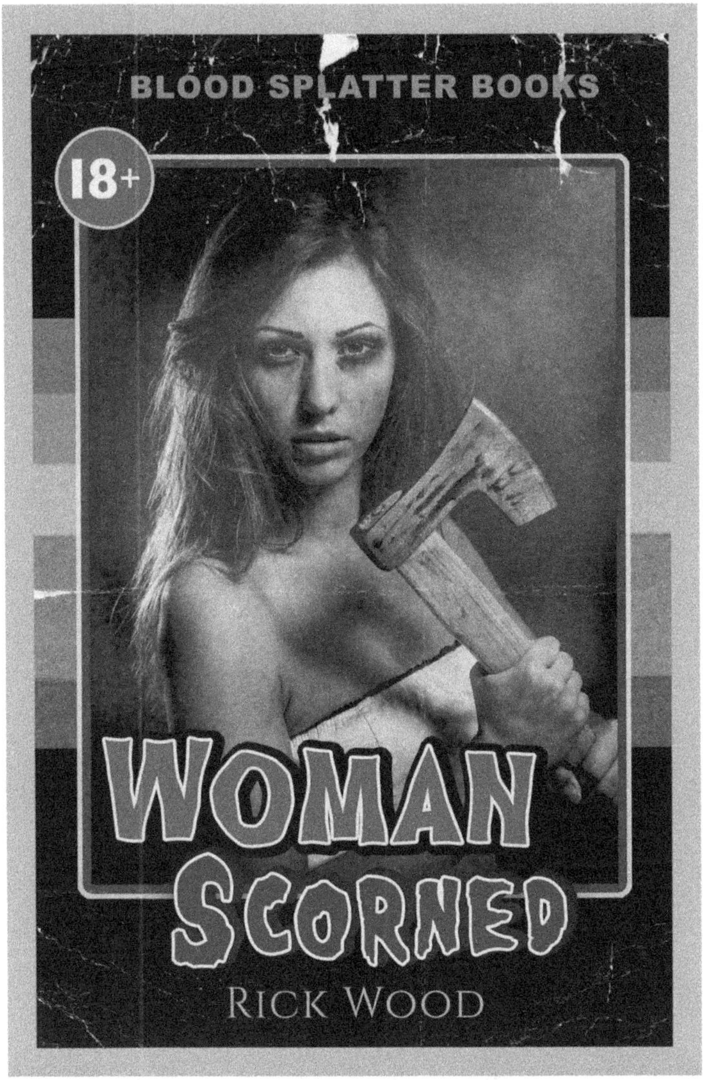
BLOOD SPLATTER BOOKS
18+
WOMAN
SCORNED
RICK WOOD

RICK WOOD

CIA ROSE BOOK ONE

WHEN THE WORLD HAS ENDED

Printed in the USA
CPSIA information can be obtained
at www.ICGtesting.com
LVHW051201181223
766713LV00029B/352/J